Mary Veronica's Egg

by
Mary Nethery

pictures by
Paul Yalowitz

Orchard Books New York

Orchard Books / A Grolier Company
95 Madison Avenue, New York, NY 10016

Manufactured in the United States of America
Printed and bound by Phoenix Color Corp. Book design by Mina Greenstein
The text of this book is set in 16 point Horley Old Style. The illustrations are colored pencil.
1 3 5 7 9 10 8 6 4 2

Library of Congress Cataloging-in-Publication Data
Nethery, Mary. Mary Veronica's egg / by Mary Nethery ; with pictures by Paul Yalowitz.
p.   cm.   Summary: Mary Veronica learns an important lesson about love while she cares
for an egg that is getting ready to hatch.
ISBN 0-531-30134-6 (trade : alk. paper).—ISBN 0-531-33134-2 (lib. bdg. : alk. paper)
[1. Eggs—Fiction. 2. Ducks—Fiction.]   I. Yalowitz, Paul, ill.   II. Title.
PZ7.N4388Mar   1999   [E]—dc21   98-35723

To my sweet sisters, Anita Louise and Gina Margaret, Beth and Alyson, and all of my fabulous sisters:

the Write Sisters—Ann Whitford Paul, Dian Curtis Regan, Helen Ketteman, Kirby Larson, Tricia Gardella, and Vivian Sathre; my Thursday Sisters—Barbara Kerley Kelly, Ellen Davidson, and Natasha Wing; my Nine-to-Five Sisters—Cathy, Cheryl, Kathy, Paulette, and Sheila; my special sister, Deb.

And, as always, to Han, the best prize of all!

—M.N.

This is dedicated to the ones I love.

—P.Y.

On Wednesday Mary Veronica found an egg sitting all alone by the pond. She'd never seen an egg like this before. It was much bigger than a chicken's egg and still warm.

Mary Veronica searched through the tall grass. She looked and looked but couldn't find its mother.

When she got home, Mary Veronica chose a small box and filled it with fluff. She added a seat belt for egg safety and a carrying strap. The egg cradle fit warm and snug up under her arm.

"Perfect," she said.

"That's a rotten egg," said her sister Mary Louise. "Poor shell color."

"It's a dinosaur egg," said her other sister, Mary Margaret. "Can I have it?"

"No," said Mary Veronica. "There's something special inside my egg—maybe an alligator! I'm going to hatch it and win the gold ribbon for Most Unusual Pet at the pet fair on Friday."

During dinner Mary Veronica had trouble cutting her meat. A brussels sprout shot off her plate and plip-plopped into the fruit compote.

Her mother sighed. "I wish you would take off that egg."

But all Mary Veronica could think about was winning the marvelous gold ribbon for Most Unusual Pet. "There's something special inside my egg," she said. "Maybe a platypus, or even a python."

"I see your rotten egg hasn't hatched yet," said Mary Louise on Thursday morning.

"It's a dinosaur egg," said Mary Margaret. "They take millions of years to hatch. Can I have it?"

"No," said Mary Veronica. "There might be a dragon lizard inside. *That* should be special enough to win the gold ribbon for Most Unusual Pet."

She colored a sign for the school bus: EGG ON BOARD. Mrs. Wriggleby drove around the lumps and holes in the road so the egg wouldn't crack.

Mary Veronica showed the egg to Mr. Puddle, her teacher.

"A science experiment!" exclaimed Mr. Puddle. "Simply maintain the egg at a temperature between ninety and one hundred degrees."

Mary Veronica set the egg on the sharing table while she collected milk money. But when she finished her job . . .

. . . the egg was gone.

Mary Veronica was distraught.

Mr. Puddle asked everyone to search the cubbies. They looked under the easels. They emptied tubs and tore apart the housekeeping corner.

Mr. Puddle found the egg in a bowl in the cooking center.

Mary Veronica put the egg safely under her arm. "This is *not* an egg for cooking," she said. "And it is *not* a science experiment."

That night Mary Veronica noticed the egg was a bit smudgy. So she gave it a bubble bath. She washed what she thought might be the top of its head.

"I'm sorry you lost your mommy," she said. Then she sang it a lullaby and tucked it into its cradle.

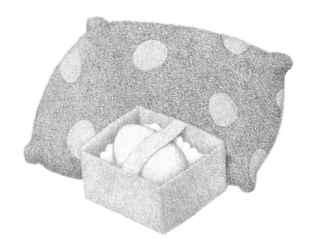

"I hope that egg doesn't break on the bus," said Mary Louise on Friday morning. "Rotten-egg slime cannot be removed with ordinary soap."

"It's a dinosaur egg," said Mary Margaret. "No wonder it hasn't hatched yet. Can I have it?"

"No," said Mary Veronica. "There's something special inside this egg, and it's going to win that gold ribbon."

When Mary Veronica got off the school bus, she went straight to the auditorium to enter her egg in the pet fair. The ribbons were extraordinary. Mary Veronica stopped to admire the marvelous gold ribbon with the frilly rosette.

She kissed the egg and placed it under a warm lamp. "It should hatch any moment," she explained to the judge.

"Can't judge anything inside of an egg," said Dr. Peepers. "Outside, yes. Inside, no."

The egg sat. Dr. Peepers peered into cage after cage, pinning ribbons here and there. He gave one ribbon to an iguana, Most Scaly, and another to a parrot, Most Congenial. Someone's spider walked away with Best Legs, and a rat grabbed Most Likely to Succeed.

Finally, there was only one ribbon left.

"AND NOW THE MOST UNUSUAL PET AWARD,"
bellowed Dr. Peepers, "for a pet of distinction—
extraordinary and special!
A zinger, a zapper, a zowzer!"

Mary Veronica grabbed her egg. "Wait!" she pleaded.
"There's something extra special inside my egg. You'll see."

Dr. Peepers looked at his watch. "Can't miss my marimba lesson. Can't wait a minute more. THE MOST UNUSUAL PET AWARD GOES TO . . . CHEE CHEE, THE HAIRLESS DOG!"

Mary Veronica drooped like a wilted flower. Everyone clapped and cheered as Chee Chee pranced about in his little tuxedo.

Mary Veronica turned off the lamp. "What if you never hatch?"
She patted the egg with her finger. Something tapped back.
Rik-tik-tik. Mary Veronica put the egg to her ear. *Rik-tik-tik.*
"My egg is hatching!" she shouted.
Everyone crowded around. The pecking grew faster. *Rik-tik-tik.*
The egg rocked. *Rik-tik-tik. Rik-tik-tik.*

Suddenly the egg cracked open.

"A dinosaur duck!" exclaimed Mary Margaret. "Can I have it?"

"Don't be dumb," said Mary Louise. "It's just a plain old duck."

"A common domestic duck," Dr. Peepers agreed.

But the duckling fastened its tiny eyes on Mary Veronica.

Zing! went Mary Veronica's heart. The baby nibbled her chin and nestled softly against her cheek.

Zap! Mary Veronica beamed.

Zowzer! She'd been right all along.

"You may be just a plain old duck," Mary Veronica cooed, and kissed the top of its head. "But you're all mine."

And finally, Mary Veronica knew just
how special the something inside
her egg had been. "You're
the best prize of all,"
she said.
"PEEP!"
squeaked
the baby.